GRuBtoWN taLes
Book One

Stinking Rich aNd Just PlaiN StiNky

or

A Diamond As Big As His Head

A bit about the author

Philip Ardagh is the award-winning author of the Eddie Dickens adventures, currently in over 30 languages. He wrote BBC radio's first truly interactive radio drama, collaborated with Sir Paul McCartney on his first children's book and is a 'regularly irregular' reviewer of children's books for the *Guardian*. Married with a son, he divides his time between Tunbridge Wells and Grubtown, where he cultivates his impressive beard.

Other children's books by Philip Ardagh published by Faber & Faber

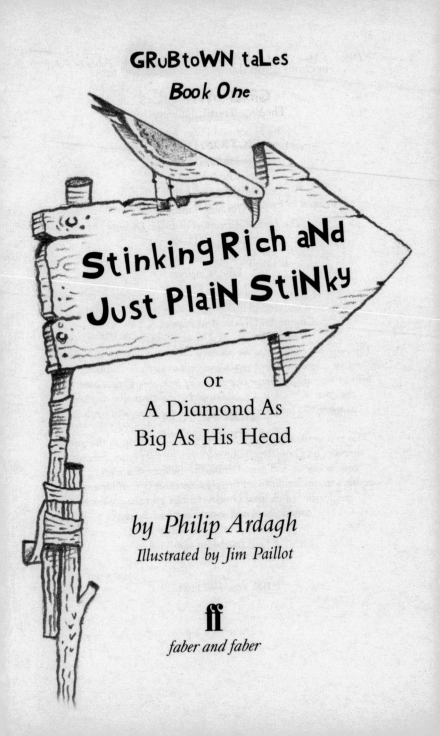

GRuBtoWN taLes
Book One

Stinking Rich aNd
Just PlaiN StiNky

or
A Diamond As
Big As His Head

by *Philip Ardagh*
Illustrated by Jim Paillot

ff

faber and faber

For SJ's Horsy,
because small things often mean the most

First published in 2009
by Faber and Faber Limited
BloomsburyHouse, 74–77 Great Russell Street,
London WC1B 3DA

Typeset by Faber and Faber Limited
Printed in England by CPI Bookmarque, Croydon

A CIP record for this book
is available from the British Library

ISBN 978–0–571–24232–0

6 8 10 9 7 5

A bit about Grubtown

You won't find Grubtown on any maps. The last time any map-makers were sent anywhere near the place they were found a week later wearing nothing but pages from a telephone directory, and calling for their mothers. It's certainly a town and certainly grubby – except for the squeaky clean parts – but everything else we know about the place comes from Beardy Ardagh, town resident and author of these tales.

GRuBtoWN taLes were made possible through the participation of the following people, animals and organisations:

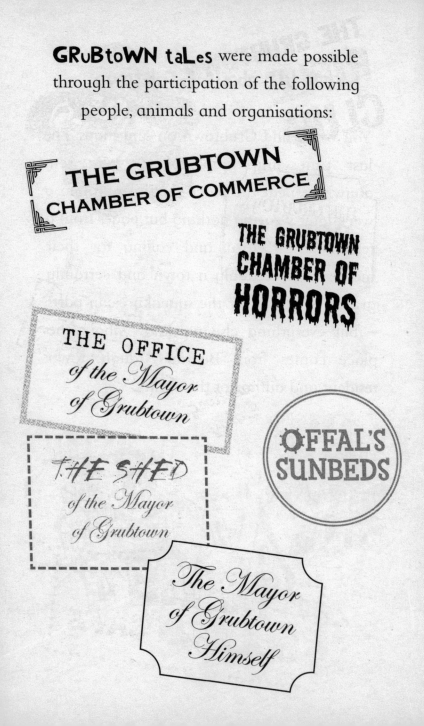

THE GRUBTOWN
CHAMBER OF COMMERCE

THE GRUBTOWN
CHAMBER OF
HORRORS

THE OFFICE
*of the Mayor
of Grubtown*

~~THE SHED~~
*of the Mayor
of Grubtown*

OFFAL'S
SUNBEDS

*The Mayor
of Grubtown
Himself*

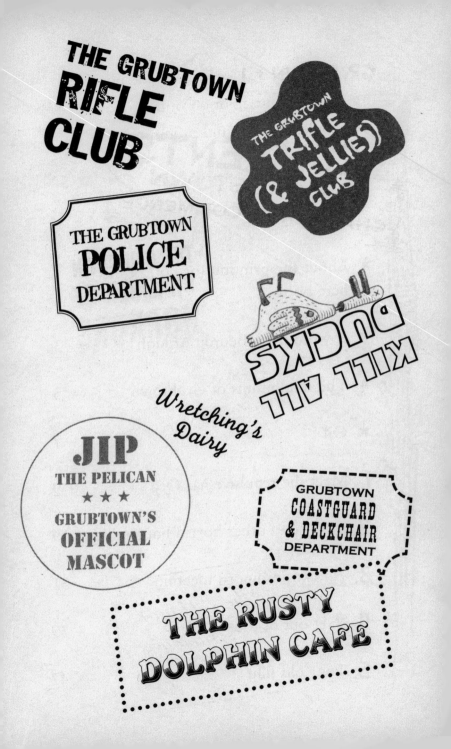

THE GRUBTOWN **RIFLE CLUB**

THE GRUBTOWN TRIFLE (& JELLIES) CLUB

THE GRUBTOWN **POLICE** DEPARTMENT

KILL ALL DUCKS

Wretching's Dairy

JIP THE PELICAN ★ ★ ★ GRUBTOWN'S **OFFICIAL MASCOT**

GRUBTOWN COASTGUARD & DECKCHAIR DEPARTMENT

THE RUSTY DOLPHIN CAFE

CONTENTS

A short message about the printing (or not) of this here book

This book was originally going to be printed by GRUBTOWN PRINTERS & CAKE DECORATORS (ESTABLISHED 1908, PROPRIETOR MR PALTRY FEEDBACK) until Beardy Ardagh (who wrote it) had a falling out with Paltry Feedback over which one of them has a more impressive beard. There is no doubt that Mr Ardagh's beard is bigger and bushier than Mr Feedback's, but Mr Feedback argues that his is more impressive because of his GREAT BIG handlebar moustache. (A handlebar moustache is a moustache which looks like

1

the handlebars of a bike, so heaven knows what they were called before bikes were invented.) Beardy Ardagh argues that a natural or 'freestyle' beard (left to do its own thing) always rates more highly than a styled beard or moustache (whipped into shape). Whoever is right or wrong, **GRUBTOWN PRINTERS & CAKE DECORATORS (ESTABLISHED 1908, PROPRIETOR MR PALTRY FEEDBACK)** didn't get to print the book. Luckily, someone else did. (Do you think they have a beard? I doubt it.)

A word from
Beardy Ardagh

You may well ask, 'Who's the hero of this tale?' And my answer would be: 'How should I know? Why are you asking me?' Not every story has a hero. Who's the hero of 'Jack and the Beanstalk', for example? Surely not that idiotic boy who sold the family cow for a handful of beans and STOLE from a giant??? Sounds more like a feather-brained thief than a hero to me. (Not that you were asking.)

Young Jilly Cheeter, Grubtown's resident duck-gatherer, certainly plays her part in this **GRuBtoWN taLe**, and her friend Mango

Claptrap does too. In fact, *his* head is the head which the diamond is as big as, so that must count for something ... But what about me? I may not be the actual hero, but it's thanks to me that you get to hear what goes on in Grubtown, so that must make me some kind of a something. Perhaps I should wear a special cape?

Come to think of it, it's probably Grubtown itself which is the hero. After all, this is a **GRuBtoWN taLe**. So enough of this nonsense, stop standing on my beard and enjoy the story. That's an order.

Beardy Ardagh

Grubtown

The inhabitants of Grubtown

At the back of the book (starting on page 135), you'll find a list of some of the people who live in Grubtown, including Jilly Cheeter and Mango Claptrap but NOT Paltry Feedback, proprietor of GRUBTOWN PRINTERS & CAKE DECORATORS (ESTABLISHED 1908) because Beardy Ardagh has said that he won't include Mr Feedback in any list anywhere, except a list of people who DON'T HAVE SUCH AN IMPRESSIVE BEARD AS HIS. (In which case, Mr Paltry Feedback would appear *right at the very top*. So there.)

Oi!

I thought I told you to get on with enjoying the story.

Beardy Ardagh●

Grubtown

Manual Org was repulsive. How repulsive? I'll tell you how repulsive Manual Org was. He once entered a competition to find the 'Most Repulsive Person in the Area at the Time' and he was disqualified . . . for being too repulsive. Would I lie to you? (Except for money.)

You know how people go on about greasy hair? Well, Manual Org's hair was so greasy that it was more grease than it was hair, so it would be more accurate to have called it *hairy grease* than greasy hair. You'd probably go

'**Yerch!**' and run away from him as fast as your little legs – or wheels – would carry you. It's hard to imagine anyone having such hairy grease on top of their head. And what a head.

Have you ever seen a really rotten potato? One that's been forgotten about and left to do its own thing?

You have?

What an exciting life you must lead. Do write and tell me about it.

(On second thoughts, DON'T. I don't want you to. If you do, I'll simply look at your letter, sneer at it like I do a worthless piece of cheese, then put it in a pile marked: IGNORE IT AND HOPE THAT IT MIGHT GO AWAY SOONER RATHER THAN LATER.)

Manual Org's head was like a rotten potato. It was lumpy, it was brownish yellow or yellowish brown (depending on which direction you were approaching him from)

and it was knobbly.

If it had been raining for a while, Manual Org often had little green shoots growing out of his ears. When the weather was really hot, the grease poured from his head running into the melted wax dripping from his ears and they combined to form something which looked like the evil half-brother of golden syrup. (*'Stay back!'*) This is the gooey liquid of nightmares. And I should know, I've had a few bad dreams about it myself.

And so to Manual Org's breath. Once, when he was in an orderly queue of people waiting for their turn to point and laugh at the village idiot, he did a burp. If this writing was to scale, it would be more of a:

I'm sorry, but there it is. Facts are facts and marmalade is stuff you spread on distant trees to keep the wasps away at picnics. His burp smelt of all the things he'd eaten that day, which included (in order of eating):

★ two-thirds of a pickled raw herring
★ a pickled onion
★ eleven gherkins
★ a fly (by mistake)
★ a fly (on purpose, because he liked the taste of the first one so much)
★ one jar of sandwich spread (one month past sell-by date)
★ a bag of monosodium glutamate
★ a packet of crisps mixed with his own toenail clippings
★ a boiled fox (road kill)
★ three peppermints (pre-sucked)

which wasn't very nice for the six people

standing downwind of him.

So let's just agree that Manual Org was repulsive. If I say much more about his repulsivosity – and, yes, I did just make that word up – you might chuck this book aside. After all, most things are more fun than thinking about Manual Org's smell and appearance, and that includes swimming in a bowl of raw liver or cleaning the underside of a garden snail. With your tongue.

I think I need a bath after all that. Just give me a few minutes.

Chapter Two
Burps and other horrid happenings

Thanks. Sorry about that. Did you miss me? I was away a little longer than I planned because I ran into Sonia Pipkin on my way to the bathroom. She's putting a window in our airing cupboard – I mean making a window in the airing cupboard wall, not literally putting one in the airing cupboard like you do with laundry (which would be plain stupid) – because I love looking at our hot-water tank in the evening, which means opening the door and letting all the heat out, which annoys the troll. Sonia wanted to know whether I want the window sill on the inside or the out . . . Anyway, I'm here now and that's what matters.

Now, where was I? Oh, yes: Manual Org burping in the queue while waiting to see the village idiot. Jilly Cheeter, a girl who was immediately in front of him, collapsed on to the person in front of *her*. Fortunately for Jilly that was Flabby Gomez who, as his name suggests, is a bit – er – flabby. He made a nice soft landing for Jilly, and Flabby Gomez hardly felt a thing on account of his rolls of flab.

Flabby Gomez is one of the nicest people I've ever had the pleasure of being trapped with in a cake shop overnight. He knits all his own clothes and doesn't always use wool. He is currently knitting his own house with two enormous knitting needles and a grant from the council.

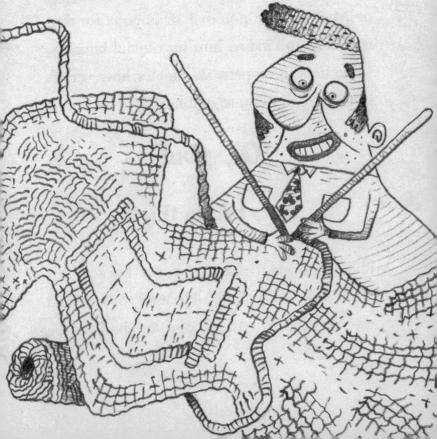

The council gives out lots of grants, mostly to Flabby Gomez. He owns this town and is in charge of grant-giving-out too. He won the town in a raffle from Big Man Gomez who owned it before him. (Flabby's brother Hacking-Cough Gomez won a tea set with two missing saucers and a cracked sugar bowl.)

Flabby Gomez's official title is the Mayor or 'Mr Mayor' if you or I, or anyone for that matter, is talking to him on official business. (If he steals your prize vegetables, however, it's still perfectly okay to call him

'Oi, you!'

or

'Dirty rotten thief!'

and to chuck a marrow at the back of his head as he runs away.) He used to be called the Worshipful Mayor and he had to be

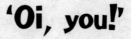

addressed (like an envelope) as '*Your Worship*', but Flabby thought that was silly, especially when he suspected that some townsfolk were deliberately calling him 'Your Warship' on account of his being as big a sea-going vessel.

Being mayor, of course, means that Flabby Gomez needn't have stood in the queue to wait his turn to taunt the village idiot.. He could have pushed his way to the front or have arranged a private taunting session in the garden shed he and his family are living in until he's completed his new house.

For those of you who think, 'In a garden shed? Don't be so ridiculous, you bearded nutter!'

I should explain that:

(a) It's not polite to call me a bearded nutter;

(b) The shed in question is rather a BIG garden shed.

At first glance, Mayor Flabby Gomez's house looks like a rather ordinary garden shed but look upwards and you'll see a spacious dwelling on eight storeys (though the Gomezes only occupy the first six). The seventh floor is used for storage and the eighth was, at the time the main events of this story happened, being used by some escaped lab rats who have extraordinarily shaggy coats of fur and are very fond of classical music – except for anything by Brahms – but their extraordinary history is for another time, in a different book.

Okay, okay, so the sadder ones amongst you are probably saying, 'If Gomez is a mayor and there are townsfolk, surely this story is set in a town and not a village . . . so why do they have a village idiot and not a town idiot?'

Firstly, let me suggest that you **GET A LIFE AND STOP BOTHERING ME WITH**

SUCH MINOR DETAILS! Secondly, let me assure you that it isn't a matter of money. Our town could afford a town idiot if we wanted one. The reason why people were queuing to see a village idiot was that the idiot had strayed from the nearest village (of Werty) and we were all out in force to show our support.

Formal Dripping, the idiot in question, rarely strays our way and it's always a big occasion when he does turn up in Grubtown which — you may have guessed — is the name of our town. Formal takes his job very seriously.

Formal not only drools brilliantly for an official idiot — you should see the permanent wet patches all the way down the front of his clothes — but he also has a permanently dripping nose (hence the name). What a skill.

So Manual Org's burp was so noxious and nasty and generally 'orrible in the fume department that the girl Jilly Cheeter collapsed on to Flabby Gomez who was doing his best to defend his own nose against the hazardous gas now heading his way.

By now the remaining members of the village-idiot queue in front of Manual Org were falling like nine-pins, gasping for air

but, unfortunately, simply inhaling more of
the poisonous burp. They clawed the air and
cried for their mummies. Mrs Awning –
second from the front, first name unknown –
managed to pull her handbag over her head
as a makeshift gas mask, and promptly ran
into the knee-high circular wall surrounding
the town well. She tipped forward into the
well itself and, after a very brief,

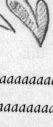

'*Aaaaaaaaaaaaaaaaaaaaaaaaaaaaaaaaaaaa aaaaaaaaaaaaaaaaaaaaaaaaaaaaaaaaaaaa aaaaaaaaaaaaaaaaaaaaaaaaaaaaaaaaaaaa aaaaaaaaaaaaaaaaaaaaaaaaaaaaaaaaaaaa aaaaaaaaaaaaaaaaaaaaaaaaaaaaaaaaaaaa aaaaaaaaaaaaaaaaaaaaaaaaaaaaaaaaaaaa aaaaaaaaaaaaaaaaaaaaaaaaaaaaaaaaaaaa aaaaaaaaaaaaaaaaaaaaaaaaaaaaaaaaaaaa aaah!*' – well, maybe not *that* brief – landed in the water with a 'HSALPS!' which should have been a 'SPLASH!' but she landed head first.

Formal Dripping, who had witnessed the whole thing, laughed like an idiot. One would have expected no less of him. This man was, and still is, a true professional.

The townsfolk rallied around in next to no time and, with the aid a of a large length of knitting Mayor Gomez had been working on, Mrs Awning was pulled from the well. Jilly Cheeter, meanwhile, was revived with a fizzy tonic that packs such a punch it's called

KNOCK OUT POW!

and has a very jazzy red and yellow label.

For many people who'd witnessed the chain of events caused by Manual Org's latest noxious burp, this was the last straw. Enough was enough.

Something Must Be Done.

Chapter Three
An extraordinary meeting

It was decided that there should be an extraordinary town council meeting. Of course, Flabby Gomez was there, dressed in his ceremonial robe which doubles as the curtain around the single polling booth used for mayoral elections. These elections take place under an age-old voting system called 'one man one vote'. You might have heard of it. (Being the owner of the town, Flabby is the one man with that one vote, and he has always voted for himself.)

Next to the mayor stood the impressive figure of the chief of police, Grabby Hanson. Grabby had been given the nickname

'Grabby' as a child – his real name is Kumquat – because, from the moment he was born, he grabbed anything and everything in sight: a toy; a baby from a pram; a TV remote from the arm of a chair; a teacher from a class; radioactive waste from a secret government underground dumping ground.

He's the best COP (Chief of Police) we've ever had in Grubtown, with the highest crime clear-up rate, because he understands the criminal mind inside out. Nine times out of ten he knows when crimes are going to take place before they've even been committed. Moments after they've been carried out, he's aware who the culprit is and what they've done with the loot. And do you know how?

Go on, guess.

Pleeeeeeeeeeeeeeeeeeeeeeeeeease.

You're right (or wrong).

Yup, it's because **90%** of crimes in Grubtown are thefts and it's Grabby Hanson himself who's done the stealing. Once he's satisfied his uncontrollable urge to take whatever it is — a priceless vase; a valuable painting; a sleeping owl — he is always racked with guilt, and arrests himself or turns himself in. He often gets himself off on a technicality before the matter comes to trial, but he always ensures that the victims get their property returned to them, and that the crime and solution are properly noted in the official records and crime statistics.

Householders who go downstairs to discover that it's Chief Hanson who's doing the thieving are always relieved. He is always so polite and apologetic. Some townsfolk don't even bother getting out of bed if they hear someone rummaging around at night. They know they'll have their silver teapot or telly returned promptly the next day.

It wasn't only adults who were at the town meeting. The children of Grubtown didn't want to miss out either, though Jilly Cheeter was actually there as part of her duty as the town's official duck-gatherer. As the job title suggests, it was — though no longer is — Jilly's job to gather together the ducks of Grubtown each evening and herd them into the Duck House where they spent their nights in relative safety away from the Foxes.

The Foxes are a family (of human beings, not foxes)

who'd moved into the town some twenty years previously. (Well, Mum and Dad had. The others were born later.) The Foxes were popular and happy-go-lucky folk until one day, during her driving test, Mrs Bunty Fox was distracted by the quack of a local duck. She claimed that this had caused her to fail the test. Small wonder she failed. She crashed the car into a ferry, having driven off the end of the jetty near The Rusty Dolphin Cafe.

After that, Bunty Fox, her husband Derek and all the little Foxes – Shaun, Mantle, Fastbuck and Garrideb – hated all the Grubtown ducks with a passion. They wrote unpleasant poems about ducks and sent them to the local papers.* They drew pictures of nasty things happening to ducks and regularly stuck these up around town (on trees and lampposts and the backs of the more slow-moving pensioners).

They even opened a shop on Cauldwell

*The Grubtown Daily Herald and The Grubtown Weekly Gerald

Street – far away from the beach, which made the rent and rates much cheaper – called **KILL ALL DUCKS** which sold nothing but home-made models of ducks involved in fatal accidents. They never sold

anything except to each other and the occasional bemused out-of-towner. And, at night, every night, the Fox family would creep out of doors with the intent of doing the ducks of Grubtown **NO GOOD**.

(I should add that Jilly had landed the job of duck-gatherer completely by accident. Her mum had sent her to the council to complain about something but she went through the wrong door. She found herself in the office of Rambo Sanskrit – the job-giver-outer – and came out with the job and a key to The Duck House around her neck.)

All the Foxes were there at the extraordinary town meeting, of course. They closed Kill All Ducks for the day, which didn't really make any difference to the business because no one (except themselves) bought much of their stuff anyway. Bunty Fox even wore a home-made T-shirt with the slogan **SAY NO TO D** on the front, and **UCKS** on the back. They planned to take the opportunity of a town gathering to fight for their cause: *getting rid of Grubtown's ducks once and for all.*

Chapter Four
'Get out of town!'

Two noticeable no-shows for the **'Something Must be Done (About Shh You-Know-Who)'** meeting were Mickey 'Steamroller' Johnson and Acrid Scorn. Mickey 'Steamroller' Johnson was in prison at the time for trying to run over Minty Glibb in **MINTY'S CAKE SHOP**. If you must know, it had to do with a white shirt, an extra jammy doughnut and Johnson having wanted to impress the future Mrs Johnson (who back then was still called Leggy Prune). Thanks to help from a passing angry mob, led by Farflung Heaps, and the intervention of Constable Gelatine – a police sergeant – Minty herself was unharmed.

Acrid Scorn wasn't in the town hall because of urgent business. He was responsible for the disposal of all the town's toxic waste. Toxic is another word for poisonous and Acrid's tanker lorries were plastered with warning symbols, including a skull-and-crossbones. When I say that Acrid Scorn was responsible for the disposal of this dangerous waste, what I actually mean was that he was *irresponsible*. But we didn't know that at the time. Most of us assumed that he wasn't at the meeting because he was one of the few people who probably didn't mind Manual Org's terrible smell and repulsive appearance. He was used to dealing with hazardous materials. Little did we know that, while the rest of us were gathering for the meeting, he was pumping gallons and gallons of dreadfully dangerous gunge out of one of his tankers into Ah-Isn't-This-A-Lovely-Spot Lake in Brambly Park.

Oh dear.

(He'd once tried pumping some gunge out to sea, but the tide had brought it straight back in again and he'd been lucky not to have been caught.)

The town hall, meanwhile, was packed. By the time Flabby Gomez banged his mayoral gavel and said, 'This meeting will come to order!', there were people sitting on chairs on people sitting on chairs and people standing on people standing on people sitting on chairs on people sitting on chairs. All the windows were open and the only thing stopping people from falling out of them was the throng of other people *outside* trying to get in them to attend the meeting.

Grubtown hadn't seen anything like it since the world-famous singer Shoona Loose came to perform a charity concert for Ex-Seaside Donkeys With A Slight Limp In One Or Both Rear Leg(s). And there'd been free orange squash at that.

When Flabby banged that gavel there was silence, except for the sound of a hacking cough coming from the mayor's brother Hacking-Cough Gomez. When the coughing stopped, Gomez got to his feet.

'Grubtown prides itself on welcoming people from all parts of the globe,' he said.

Everyone clapped and cheered.

'We welcome people from all walks of life.'

There was more cheering.

'We welcome people whatever their body shape –'

Cheers.

'Hairstyles –'

'What about baldies?' shouted Luminous Shard (a mechanic who is as bald as anything that's completely bald).

Flabby Gomez glared at him. Shard hid behind the chair leg of the man sitting on him.

'Whatever their hairstyles,' the mayor repeated, 'their height, shoe-size and clothing. We open our arms to each and every one of them . . . But —' He paused. Everyone had been waiting for the 'but'. '— But in return we ask that they clean their ears out once in a while.'

Cheers!

'We ask that they wash their hair with shampoo —'

'And conditioner!' shouted Mrs Awning.

'And conditioner,' agreed Flabby Gomez with an approving nod, which annoyed Luminous Shard more than a little bit, 'at least once a month, and that they brush their teeth a least once in a lifetime.'

There was a burst of wild cheering this time.

'Should any citizen of Grubtown fail to do all of the above when requested, the council reserves the right to banish them from Grubtown for ever!'

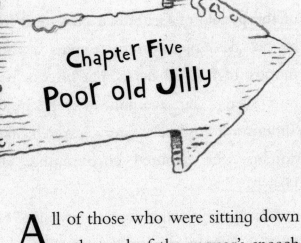

Chapter Five
Poor old Jilly

All of those who were sitting down at the end of the mayor's speech tried to jump to their feet to cheer, which was impossible with the people on top of them . . . and the townsfolk at the very top of the pile were unable to leap about either, because their heads were squashed up against the ceiling. So everyone waved their arms about a bit instead.

The floor was then opened to public comment, which means that people were allowed to have their say. As planned, Mantle Fox leapt up. He argued that, with so many of the people of Grubtown present, it might be an ideal opportunity to pass a council motion to ban all ducks, but he was booed into silence by everyone except brothers Shaun and Fastbuck, sister Garrideb and his parents who shouted encouraging 'Hear! Hear!'s.

Mrs Awning called for the town well to be filled in immediately as a safety hazard, and Leggy Prune urged the council to grant her future husband Mickey Johnson an early release from jail if he promised never to flatten any cake shops with his steamroller ever again. Ever.

Four of the seven Grumbly girls burst into their well-known rendition of '**Don't Stick That Chicken Up Your Jumper, Uncle Harry**', and Carlo Monte took the opportunity to announce that he'd be opening his illegal off-shore gambling den aboard *The Crooked Sixpence* a week on Thursday.

The reason why he was happy to make an announcement so publicly within the earshot of the mayor and the chief of police was because the mayor actually owned *The Crooked Sixpence* and the chief of police's sister, Pageant, was to be in charge of all on-board refreshments.

It was Jilly Cheeter who asked the awkward question: 'Who's going to tell Manual Org?'

There was an uncomfortable silence, which is just like an ordinary silence, except that everyone feels uncomfortable.

'I believe,' said Grabby Hanson, 'that this responsibility lies with the town's official duck-gatherer.'

'Why me?' demanded Jilly. 'What does it have to do with gathering ducks?'

'The chief's right,' announced Mayor Gomez. 'As duck-gatherer you're one of the first people up every morning, to let the ducks

out of the Duck House . . . and Org Manual
needs to be told first thing.'

'Then why not get the chief to set his
alarm?' Jilly argued.

'It's in your job description.'

'No it isn't,' Jilly protested. 'You just chose
me because I was silly enough to open my
big mouth and –'

'Rambo?' said Flabby Gomez, calling for
Rambo Sanskrit, the job-giver-outer.

'Yes, Mr Mayor?'

'Isn't "telling Manual Org" in Miss
Cheeter's job description?'

'It is now,' nodded the job-giver-outer.

'See?' said Flabby, with a certain
satisfaction.

''S'not fair,' mumbled Jilly Cheeter, but she
knew better than to keep complaining.

'Excellent!' said Mayor Flabby Gomez.
'You will tell Manual Org the new town rules
tomorrow morning before breakfast.' He

banged his gavel again. 'Our work here is done.'

It was even harder getting everyone *out* of the town hall than it had been getting them in. Several sheep grazing on the green were injured (none seriously) and Jip, the town mascot – a pelican – suffered a suspected bruised upper beak. Mrs Awning fell down the town hall steps, head first into a litter bin. She emerged unharmed but shaken, with a

half-empty low-fat strawberry yoghurt pot stuck to her forehead. Marley Gripe (the town's sign painter) became entangled in a red fire bucket (filled with sand) from the foyer, and a smallish boy named Mango Claptrap found an **I've Been To Grubtown!** souvenir ball-point pen somehow lodged in his ear. It was Jilly Cheeter who helped to pull it out.

'Thanks, Jilly,' he said.

'My pleasure,' said Jilly, handing her friend the pen. 'You might as well keep it, Mango.'

The two kids walked down the steps together. Although they are roughly the same age – they were born in the same year but Jilly's birthday is 14th April and Mango's is the 24th Umph – she is quite a bit taller than he is. (In Grubtown we've adopted a slightly different calendar to the one you might be used to.) Because Miss Cheeter isn't particularly tall for her age, this means that Mango must be quite small for his. And his shorts make him look much younger.

'Hard luck having to tell Mr Org,' said Mango.

'Thanks,' said Jilly. 'I feel sorry for him. It's not his fault that he's utterly repulsive.'

'Well,' said Mango Claptrap cautiously, 'it *is* partly his fault, actually. He could wash and brush and stuff now and again, couldn't he?'

'I suppose,' Jilly agreed.

They climbed over two of the Grumbly girls who were somehow entangled in a town-hall chair by a fire hydrant.

'Isn't it time you rounded up the ducks?' asked Mango.

Jilly looked at her left wrist, where she'd wear a watch if she had one, then glanced up at the town hall clock. 'You're right,' she said. 'Want to help?' She knew the answer would be 'I sure do!' Mango Claptrap loved helping with the duck gathering.

'I sure do!' he said. See? He didn't disappoint her.

They made their way across the grass covering the middle of the town hall square and down the alleyway between the public lending library and Offal's Sunbeds. Emerging from the other end of the alley, Jilly and Mango took a few turns down various streets – passing Acrid Scorn in one of his filthy hazardous-waste tankers, a guilty grin on his face — until they came to The Duck House. You may imagine that The Duck House was some custom-built house not unlike a giant chicken coop and made from wood, but you'd be wrong, wrong, wrong, wrong, WRONG. Hang your head in shame for such foolishness, my ignorant reader! This building was truly amazing.

Chapter Six
An amazing find

The Duck House used to be the Governor's Residence back in the days when Grubtown had a governor, though what he was governor *of* had long been forgotten. (Such forgetting had something to do with the mists of time, some mislaid index cards in the local history archive, and the Great Memory Loss of '67, which most people had forgotten about by '68.) It's a very impressive building with pillars and a portico and lots of fine architectural features which make big fans of such

fine architectural features go '**Oooh!**' and
'**Aaaaah!**'. Only now it was full of straw and
pond weed and was the nightly home of

Grubtown's ever-growing duck population.

Jilly had a special wooden whistle called a duck-call which she blew into every evening. It made a very convincing quacking sound and attracted the attention of the ducks who knew that it meant: **FOOD** and **TIME FOR BED**. Sometimes, the ducks all ambled home in next to no time. Other times, there were stragglers and those who most definitely didn't want to go to The Duck House but to stay out late to drink pond water, splash about in the sea, or to hang with their friends.

That particular evening, the ducks were behaving very well indeed and the Cheeter girl and the Claptrap boy had little trouble herding them through the front door. They were only interrupted once and that was by Fastbuck and Mantle Fox. Mantle was holding a placard which read: **WE HATE DUCKS AND DON'T** and Fastbuck was holding one which read: **YOU FORGET IT!** and they jeered at the children as they led the ducks to safety.

'I don't think the Foxes are very nice people,' said Mango.

'Nobody thinks the Foxes are very nice people. Except for the Foxes themselves,' said Jilly. 'I bet Mrs Fox would have failed her driving test anyway, quacking duck or no quacking duck.' She said this loud enough for Fastbuck and Mantle to hear.

Fastbuck Fox was so enraged about what the Cheeter girl had just said about his mother, Bunty, that he took a big bite out the nearest thing which happened to be his brother's placard. It didn't taste very nice, so he spat it out, and the two Fox boys stomped off home.

They actually passed my house on the way. They were muttering so loudly that I was forced to open my study window and throw the nearest thing to hand at them.

I also tried to shout, 'Be quiet, I'm trying to write!' but my beard got in the way.

Unfortunately the nearest thing to (both) hand(s) was my typewriter, and I'm not very good at throwing anyway. I missed them by so much that you wouldn't have guessed that I was even aiming at them. The typewriter landed in the front garden with a pathetic *FLUMPH*. Now it smells of compost and the letter 'd' – as in 'duck' – keeps jamming, bringing us neatly back to The Duck House.

The Duck House is even more impressive inside than out. The

entrance hall alone has marble pillars, a marble floor and a beautiful staircase sweeping down (or up, depending on whether you're coming or going). There are statues in alcoves, there are panels and even built-in portraits of stern-looking men and women from yesteryear looking down (never up) with disapproval. And they had much to disapprove of because, when Jilly Cheeter was the duck-gatherer, just about every surface was covered with straw and duck feathers and the whole place smelled of *duck*.

If you're thinking that The Duck House sounds like just the grand sort of place you'd expect Mayor Flabby Gomez to make his official home, you'd be right. If you're wondering why he didn't live there, I'll tell you. Most people thought – and many still think – that The Duck House was haunted. Rather strangely, it's generally agreed that the ghosts aren't the ghosts of people. Or even the ghosts of animals. The ghosts that haunted The Duck House were thought to be the ghosts of enormous vegetables.

Mrs Awning was once found early one morning wedged in the old rubber tyre in Brambly Park which the local children use as a swing. She was foaming at the mouth and babbling deliriously. It was only after a cup of weak tea and one of Minty Glibb's (jammy) doughnuts, that she was able to tell

Dr Fraud that she'd been chased by the shimmering form of a giant marrow.

Sonia Pipkin – the builder who's currently doing some work on my airing cupboard – claims that she was walking past The Duck House one winter's evening when, through an upstairs window, she saw the ghostly figure of a carrot pacing up and down. And carrots don't have legs. (Spooky!)

Informative Boothe, who seems to know a great deal

about everything except horse racing, says that there have been sightings of everything from ghostly runner beans to Brussels sprouts. The most chilling tale he tells involves a missing puppy and a bag of ghostly frozen peas, but I won't repeat it here in case it makes you burst into tears and blow your nose on this book. (I'm only thinking of your own well-being. And the book's.)

Flabby Gomez isn't the most superstitious person I've ever met, except that he never walks under ladders (because he generally won't fit) but The Duck House was somewhere he certainly used to steer clear of.

Jilly had never seen a ghost in the house, or anywhere else for that matter. Neither had Mango Claptrap. As for the ducks, I'm afraid there's no way of knowing, but they certainly seemed to like their home. The duck-gatherer *before* Jilly, however, had not only fled the house one evening, but also Grubtown. And he never came back. He was last seen on a stolen bicycle, pedalling frantically to the town's limits, shouting, 'The cabbages! The cabbages!' Enough said.

The evening after the extraordinary town meeting when Jilly and Mango were just finishing off putting the last of the ducks to bed, there was a terrible CRASH upstairs. Without a single worry about ghostly vegetables between them, they dashed up the stairs to find out what had caused it and whether any of the ducks had been injured.

They soon found what the trouble was.

'Wow!' said Jilly Cheeter.

'Blimey!' said Mango Claptrap.

There, on the floor in the middle of the ballroom, lay an enormous chandelier, surrounded by an explosion of crystal baubles and ceiling plaster.

They looked up to where it had pulled free of its fixing.

'It's lucky we weren't standing underneath it when it fell!' said Mango.

'Or we'd be strawberry jam!' marvelled Jilly.

They went over to inspect the damage more closely. There didn't appear to be any ducks involved. The chandelier was so heavy that it had badly damaged the ballroom floor. They peered between the broken floorboards.

'What's that?' Mango pointed.

'What?' asked Jilly.

'That glinting thing?' asked Mango.

'There are hundreds of glinting things,' said Jilly. 'Thousands! There are bits of shattered chandelier everywhere.'

'I know,' said Mango. 'That's why I'm standing on tip-toe . . . But none of those glinty things are glinting quite like *that* glinty thing.'

Jilly Cheeter peered through the hole more closely. 'You're right,' she said.

They decided to sweep aside as much of the broken crystal as possible before trying to get to whatever it was that was winking and blinking at them just out of reach.

The fallen chandelier was far too big and heavy for them to shift so they swept around it with a couple of the brooms Jilly usually used to sweep up the duck feathers and dirty straw.

'Do you think that's clear enough?' asked Mango.

'Yes,' said Jilly. 'You can get it out, whatever it is, because you saw it first.'

'Thanks,' said Mango. He bent down and reached in through the hole in the floorboards.

It was a diamond. A very big diamond. An

absolutely **enormous** diamond. This
diamond was **huge**. This diamond was
gigantic. It was COLOSSAL.
It was **MAMMOTH**.
It was **GARGANTUAN**.
This diamond was by no means small.

Chapter Seven
Blimey!

'Wow!' said Jilly Cheeter, staring at the diamond Mango Claptrap was holding in both hands.

'Blimey!' said Mango.

'Do you think it's real?'

'Real what?'

'A real diamond?' said Jilly.

'It looks more diamondy than the chandelier crystals that are cut to look diamondy,' said Mango.

Jilly unhooked one of the undamaged crystal baubles dangling from the fallen chandelier and held it up to the light. Then she looked back at the diamond. 'You're right,' she said.

'I know how we can find out,' said Mango.

'By asking Lefty Scorn?' asked Jilly. Lefty Scorn (Acrid's brother) is the proprietor of Scorn's, Grubtown's laundrette and jewellery shop. People go in there and try on jewellery while waiting for their clothes to wash and dry.

'No!' said Mango. 'My dad says that he's a swindler and a cheat.'

'Only at card games and *I'll Tickle Thomas*,' said Jilly. (*I'll Tickle Thomas* is the most popular game in Grubtown. It's quite difficult to cheat at, but Lefty Scorn has had a lot of practice over the years.) 'He's supposed to be very honest when it comes to valuing jewels, though. He has a certificate to prove it.' Jilly was right. In the jewellery section of Scorn's is a glass counter stuffed full of jewels and on the wall behind it is a framed certificate (with a magnificent seal at the bottom) which reads:

This is to certify that

LEFTY SCORN Esq.

is very honest when it comes to certifying jewels though.

and is signed with some very impressive signatures from the president and chairman of the Laundrette and Jewellers' Association.

'Huh!' said Mango indignantly. 'Huh! My dad once found some rare dark red gems in chilli sauce in an unlabelled tin in the back of a kitchen cabinet and Lefty Scorn said that they were nothing more than kidney beans!'

'Maybe they *were* nothing more than kidney beans,' suggested Jilly.

'I hadn't thought of that,' admitted Mango.

The truth be told – and I generally tell the truth except when I'm lying – Mango's dad, Furl Claptrap has a bit of a reputation around town for being, how shall I put it, not **TOO** bright. Now, I have a reputation for being a bit **TOO** bearded, so I'm not saying that everyone in Grubtown is a fair-minded citizen . . . but they're probably right about Furl. When God, or Mother Nature or Charles Darwin, or whoever it was, was handing out brains, I expect Furl Claptrap had nipped out of the room to scratch his bottom or something. And came back too late.

'How do you think we can tell whether this is a real diamond or not?' asked Jilly.

'You can cut glass with a diamond,' said Mango Claptrap. 'So let's give it a go!'

He lugged the diamond over to the window in both hands, with Jilly hot on his heels. It wasn't every day you found a diamond-shaped thingy which may turn out to be the real thing! Mango managed to hold the tip of it against a pane of raindrop-splattered glass. There was a scratching sound and, sure enough, it left a mark.

'Wow!' said Jilly Cheeter.

'Blimey!' said Mango Claptrap. 'The genuine article! What do you think we should do?'

'Do?'

'Do?' said Mango. 'I mean, I found it but that doesn't make it mine, does it? I mean finders keepers losers weepers isn't an actual proper law, is it?'

'No, you're right,' agreed Jilly.

'So what do we do?'

'Well,' said Jilly. 'I'm the official Grubtown duck-gatherer and I work for the council and The Duck House is official Grubtown property, so I suppose I should tell Rambo Sanskrit. He did give me the job in the first place.'

'But can you trust him?' asked the Claptrap boy.

'Trust him? Why shouldn't I trust him?'

'Because grown-ups can act a bit funny when money is involved.'

'Hmm.'

'And I imagine that a diamond as big as my head is worth piles and piles of money.'

'You have a point there,' agreed Jilly. 'I think we should go straight to the mayor himself.'

'Right!' said Mango. 'Perhaps he'll give us a reward.'

'A finder's fee!' nodded Jilly Cheeter. She'd read about a hot-air balloonist who'd been given a finder's fee for all the hats and scarves and wigs he'd retrieved from the tops of the trees in Brambly Park following a particularly windy spell of weather. It had been front-page news in one of the local papers.* (The following week I'd found a missing child in my beard. She must have been blown in there. I don't want you to think that my beard's particularly big. It's just that the child was particularly small.)

'If we do get a reward, I'll share it with you,' said Mango. 'I mean, if it wasn't for you letting me help you with the ducks, I'd never have found it.'

* *The Grubtown Daily Herald* and
The Grubtown Weekly Gerald

'Thanks, Mango,' beamed a happy Jilly. 'Can I hold it?'

'Sure,' he said, passing it over. 'It was getting a bit heavy anyway.'

Jilly managed to hold up the massive diamond to the light. She found it hard to believe that this was a chunk of carbon. Yes, it had been beautifully cut and beautifully polished, but it was still just carbon, like the black bits on burnt toast. Weren't the charcoal biscuits her dad gave their dog Harvey made from carbon too?

Weird.

She stared deep into the stone . . . and hundreds of Manual Orgs – some of them upside-down – stared back at her.

Chapter Eight
Another big surprise

'**W**oaaaaah!' wailed Jilly Cheeter. 'You frightened me!' She lowered the diamond.

'Sorry!' said Manual Org, picking at one of the scabs or boils or whatever it was on his face. He was standing in the doorway to the ballroom. His coat looked like it had been run over several times by something leaving muddy tyre tracks. On his feet were a pair – I use the term loosely – of non-matching

79

footwear. On his left foot was a boot, with the upper part separating from the sole. On his right foot was a patent-leather brogue, that appeared to have been dipped in dung. The overall effect was, you guessed it, repulsive.

They could smell him from there.

'What are you doing in here?' demanded Jilly.

'It's raining,' Org replied.

'What's that got to do with anything, Mr

Org?' asked Mango Claptrap, sidling up next to Jilly.

'I don't like getting wet,' said Org. His breath smelled of something very dead locked in a trunk.

'You're not allowed in here,' said Jilly. 'The Duck House is for ducks and council employees only.'

'What about him?' asked Manual Org, pointing at Mango Claptrap with one of the most repulsive fingernails imaginable. The nail itself was a horrible yellow all the way through, its tip torn and jagged. Beneath the nail was what looked like a small flowerbed of soil with things in it. Possibly *living* things.

'Mango's helping me,' said Jilly.

'Then can't I help too?' asked Manual Org.

'All the ducks are inside now, thank you,' said Jilly Cheeter.

Mango gave Jilly a nudge. 'Why not tell

him,' he said, out of the corner of his mouth.

'Tell him what?' asked Jilly out of the corner of hers.

'About the town meeting. Best get it over with.'

'What about the town meeting?' asked Manual Org. He had a finger in his ear and was violently jiggling it, causing flakes of something to fall from the sides of his nose.

'The council took a vote,' said Jilly, still not sure that she'd be able to come out and tell him everything at once. How did you tell someone that nobody wanted them around?

'Basically, Mr Org,' said Mango Claptrap very bravely, 'the town has voted you out of town. You have to leave –'

'Unless you clean up your act,' Jilly quickly added, in an effort to soften the blow.

'My act?' asked Org.

'Well, *yourself*, actually,' said Jilly. Her voice was hushed.

'In what way?'

'I think they'd like you to wash your skin and your hair and your clothes and to brush your teeth and under your fingernails and to gargle loads of mouthwash, Mr Org,' said Mango.

'Really?' said Manual Org.

'Really,' said Mango.

Jilly Cheeter just nodded.

'But I'm an eccentric trillionaire,' said Manual Org. 'Aren't eccentric trillionaires supposed to dress and behave how they like?'

'Maybe in their own house . . .' said Jilly a little doubtfully.

'But I live in a tree,' said Manual Org.

'Oh,' said Jilly. 'I didn't know you didn't have a house.'

'I didn't say I didn't have a house. I said that I live in a tree.'

'Are you really an eccentric millionaire?' asked Mango Claptrap.

'*Trillionaire*,' Org corrected him. 'Oh yes, I could buy this town several times over, if Flabby wanted to sell it, that is.'

In case you're wondering, a trillion is a one and twelve noughts or, to put it another way: **1,000,000,000,000 . . .** which is a lot when you're talking about money in particular. It's enough to make greedy men dribble. (Excuse me while I go and wash my beard.)

What Mango had thought was an eyebrow turned out to be a centipede and was now wandering aimlessly around Manual Org's face. Org didn't seem to notice.

'You'd rather walk around all smelly and dirty and live in a tree?' asked Mango.

'That's about the sum of it,' Manual Org nodded, causing a slick of grease to inch further down his lank locks of hair. 'Except, sometimes when it's raining.'

Mango Claptrap suddenly had a thought

and it was quite a high-quality thought at that. 'How did you get in here, Mr Org? Once the last duck was in, I'm sure I locked the door. I'm one-hundred-per-cent positive I did, in fact.' He fingered the key Jilly had handed him.

'I used my key, of course,' said Manual Org.

'*Your* key?' asked Jilly Cheeter. 'Since when did you have a key?'

'Since I was a child and Daddikins thought I was old enough to have one.'

Jilly Cheeter gasped. 'This didn't used to be your house, by any chance, did it?'

'No,' said Manual Org.

'Oh,' said Jilly Cheeter and Mango Claptrap.

'Nothing *used-to-be* about it. It still *is* my house.'

The children's gobs were well and truly smacked. (In other words, they were

gobsmacked.) 'Then why did you let the council take it over and use it to house the ducks?' asked Jilly.

Manual Org shrugged. 'They didn't know it was anybody's and I don't mind sharing, I suppose. And I like ducks.'

'But this used to be the governor's house,' said Mango.

'Exactly,' said Org, 'and my great-great-grandfather was the last governor.'

'Of what?' asked Jilly. 'Grubtown?'

Manual Org shook his head. Something hard and crisp fell out of an ear and rolled

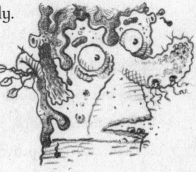

across the ballroom floor. 'Of the Grubtown Bank and Overseas Diamond Mining Company.'

'Diamond mining?!' said Jilly and Mango together.

'Yes, you know,' said Manual Org pointing to the huge diamond still in Jilly Cheeter's hands. 'Digging things like that out of the earth. My family owned the bank and the mines.'

'This is incredible,' said Mango Claptrap.

'Unbelievable,' said Jilly.

'But true,' said Manual Org.

'Which means that this diamond belongs to you,' said Jilly Cheeter, holding up the precious treasure.

Manual shrugged again. This time, nothing appeared to fall off or out of him. 'Yes,' he said, 'but what would I want with it? I'm a trillionaire already.'

'But can you prove any of this?'

'Maybe,' said Manual Org. 'Maybe not. But I certainly don't want to leave town. People are so friendly here.'

'Friendly?' said Jilly Cheeter. 'They've all ganged up on you and want you to leave!'

'If only someone had mentioned before that they don't like my appearance.'

'You'd have done something about it?'

'No, but at least I'd know where I stood. Or *should* have stood . . . Downwind of them by the sound of it.'

A duck waddled into the room between Manual's legs. They seemed to know each other.

'Hello, Orlando,' said Org.

'Quack,' said the duck.

'How come I've never run into you in here before?' asked Jilly.

'I didn't want you to see me before,' said Manual Org.

Jilly suddenly remembered when she'd

smelled some pretty dreadful smells in the house: smells which she'd put down to a combination of used straw, duck poo and old building. She now realised that there had been a slight Manual-Org-y tinge to them.

'Then why don't you mind us seeing you now, Mr Org?' asked Mango Claptrap, who hadn't moved away from Jilly's side since Org had appeared in the doorway.

'Because I saw you from outside when you held the diamond up to the window, and that changes everything. I thought we needed to have a little chat.'

Chapter Nine
A Secret f-f-fear

Now, it would be an exaggeration to say that the more Jilly and Mango talked to Manual Org the more they got used to his repulsive appearance and smell. That would be a bit like saying that I got used to having that salamander living in my beard for a while. I never got over the inconvenience, just some of the *shock*. You can never get used to a long-tailed amphibian taking up residence in your

facial hair, take my word for it. It was most off-putting and not in the least bit funny. (Not that I ever caught the creature laughing at me.)

What both Jilly and Mango agreed afterwards was that, despite being more repulsive than a garlic-belching swamp with extra dreadfulness, Mr Org seemed nice. And they felt sorry for him.

It may seem odd feeling sorry for a man with more money than he knew what to do with but perhaps that was a part of *why* they felt sorry for him.

'You don't want people to know about you being a trillionaire and having piles of diamonds and stuff?' Jilly Cheeter asked Manual Org when he'd finished speaking.

'That's right.'

'But you *do* want to stay in Grubtown.'

'Of course,' he replied. 'It's always been my home.'

'Whereas the grown-ups in Grubtown want you either to wash or to leave town, and – unlike you – they're interested in money,' said Mango.

'Well, most of them, anyway,' said Jilly Cheeter, impressed with Mango's use of the word 'whereas'.

Manual Org gave a slimy nod. Something glooped from his lank hair to the floor with a **floooop**.

'Well, I reckon one way which you could just-about absolutely positively guarantee that everyone would be delighted if you stayed would be to give every grown-up a free pair of gold-framed spectacles with

rose-tinted lenses and a built-in solid platinum clothes peg to clip over their noses –'

'That's a great idea!' said Jilly. 'Everyone loves an expensive gift, and seeing you through the spectacles would not only make you look all rosy –'

'While the clothes peg would block out the – er – smell –' Mango pointed out.

'But it would also give the townsfolk a warm feeling towards you for being so generous. If they chose to sell the specs to pay for a conservatory or a home cinema system, then they couldn't really complain if they didn't like looking at you without them, now could they?'

'But then they'd know about my being amazingly rich,' said Manual Org.

'But what I don't understand is why you want to keep it a secret,' said Jilly. She had crouched down on to the bare floorboards and the duck Manual Org had called Orlando was now sitting on her lap.

'I want people to like me for who I am. Not for my money.'

'But *nobody* likes you!' Mango Claptrap blurted out before guiltily adding: 'Well, almost nobody.'

Manual Org frowned. The furrows in his forehead were so filled with grime that they looked like a recently ploughed field. 'You do have a point there,' he said. 'Perhaps I could give them each *a bag of money* as well as the gold spectacles –?'

'With built-in platinum clothes pegs,' Mango reminded him.

'Great idea!' said Jilly Cheeter, though inside she was feeling a little unsure. Buying friends didn't seem a proper solution somehow.

It was getting darker and darker out and the rain was lashing against the windows of The Duck House. 'It's time I went home,' she said.

'Me too,' said Mango.

'Let's meet again tomorrow,' said Manual Org. 'In the meantime, do you promise to say nothing about finding the diamond or what we talked about tonight?'

'We promise,' said Jilly Cheeter and Mango Claptrap.

'Quack,' said Orlando. Perhaps she thought that she was supposed to promise too.

They all left The Duck House together. Manual Org locked the front door with the key he'd had since he was a child. Mango Claptrap handed back Jilly's key, which he'd been wearing on a string around his neck. They sheltered under the impressive porch.

'I hate the rain,' said Org. He didn't say 'I hate the rain' in the way you or I might say 'I hate the rain' (if we hated rain). This wasn't a casual 'I-don't-like-wet-weather' kind of a comment. Manual Org said 'I hate the rain' in the way you might say 'I hate slugs!' if you'd just discovered them eating your prize marrow, having already eaten their way through your peas, carrots, runner beans and favourite aunt. He said it with a VENGEANCE.

A thought popped into Jilly Cheeter's mind like one of those annoying diagrams. It went something like this:

She nudged Mango in the ribs. He glared at her. 'H-e-'s a-f-r-a-i-d o-f w-a-t-e-r,' she silently mouthed, good and slowly.

He frowned then nodded. 'Mr Org,' he asked innocently, 'why do you hate rain so much?'

Manual Org thought a while before answering. 'Water washes away love,' he said in a faraway voice, staring into the darkness. Pulling the top of his coat over his head, he ran into the night. 'Tomorrow,' he shouted back through the rain. 'Remember. We'll talk again tomorrow.'

Chapter Ten
Making a splash

The next morning came as next mornings usually do, and the sky was sky blue, filled with the usual squawking seagulls. (The seagulls are one of the very few things I dislike about Grubtown. The young ones swark like babies being bothered by a baby-botherer, and the adult birds try to steal your food and poo everywhere. And you can't turn their volume down or force them to wear nappies.)

Mango climbed over his sleeping brother, Vestige, and pulled on a pair of shorts. Whatever the weather, whatever the season, Claptrap wears shorts. It doesn't matter whether there's snow up to his eyeballs or it's raining Great Danes and Maine Coons, Mango Claptrap wears shorts. I'm not sure I'd recognise him in long trousers. I sometimes wonder whether he'll still be in shorts when he's an adult.

Stopping off for a quick bowl of **Guzzle Snaps** in the kitchen, he was out of the squeaky-hinged, ill-fitting back door before his mum could ask whether he'd washed behind both ears.

He met Jilly Cheeter outside Minty's Cake Shop. She had her head buried in a cream bun that was at least as much cream as bun. 'Want a bite?' she asked, emerging from behind the bun with a Father-Christmas-like cream moustache and beard.

'No thanks,' said Mango, with a shake of the head. 'Let's get going.'

Soon they arrived at the prearranged time at the prearranged spot at Brambly Park, passing Ah-Isn't-This-A-Lovely-Spot Lake which looked an almost-too-good-to-be-true blue that morning. They also passed a tall handsome man humming a tuneful 'top-of-the-morning-to-you' tune. That was me, in case you hadn't already guessed.

After a few minutes, Manual Org appeared at the edge of the trees fringing the park. 'You came,' he said.

'Of course we came,' said Mango.

'Sure we did,' said Jilly Cheeter. 'So now that we're here, what do you want to discuss, Mr Org?'

They sat on a bench, with Manual Org in

the middle. It was a memorial bench. It had a plaque on it remembering Mayor Flabby Gomez's father Big Man Gomez. Most people in Grubtown had been afraid of Big Man Gomez when he was alive. (He's much quieter now that he's dead.) Even today they steer clear of his memorial benches, unless there's nowhere else to sit. It didn't bother these three, though. They had important matters to discuss.

'Back in the days before I called myself Manual Org,' said Manual Org, 'I fell in love with a girl called Quince. She didn't love me. Quite the opposite in fact.'

'She hated you?' asked Jilly.

'The opposite of love isn't hate,' said Manual Org.

'It isn't?'

'No.'

'When you really love someone, you think about them all the time. When you really hate someone, you think about them all the time too. The opposite of love is indifference.'

'Indifference?' asked Jilly. 'What's that?'

'It means that Quince hardly knew I existed. I don't think she ever thought about me when she wasn't with me, and she was only with me – to talk to – two or three times.'

'But you loved her?' asked Mango Claptrap. He had a great-aunt called

Quince. She looked like a pickled walnut.

'With all my heart,' said Org. 'And there was nothing I could do about it.'

'Back then, did you – er –?'

'I washed and shampooed and brushed and gargled and was minty fresh all over, yes.'

The truth be told, both Jilly Cheeter and Mango Claptrap found a minty-fresh young pre-Manual-Org Manual Org hard to imagine. *Very* hard to imagine.

'But I was shy. I spent most of my time at home, leading a pampered but lonely existence. I spent much of every day learning to count piles of money – coins and notes – or to grade diamonds.'

'Grade?'

'Sort them by size and quality. On Fridays, my father would come home early from his club so that he could take me to his upstairs-study window and personally teach me to look down my nose at the common townsfolk,' said Org. 'So I wasn't very good at talking to people . . . particularly not a girl I was in love with. Then, one day, I rescued Quince's pet rabbit –'

'Rabbit?' asked Mango. His Great-Aunt Quince loved rabbits. On very special occasions, she even used to dress as one.

'Rabbit, and she hugged me and kissed me on the cheek. I wanted that kiss to stay there for ever,' said Manual Org, 'so I never washed again.'

'You haven't washed since that day?'

'Correct.'

'And what happened to Quince?'

'She moved away. Her parents won a very popular radio quiz show of the day called *Would You Like To Win A Big House, A Big Car and A Truckload of Cash?*. They scooped the jackpot and left Grubtown behind them. I haven't seen her since.'

'But you still have that kiss on your cheek somewhere under those layers of dirt?' asked Mango Claptrap.

Manual Org nodded.

Mango Claptrap's great-aunt's parents had won a very popular radio quiz show of the day called *Would You Like To Win A Big House, A Big Car and A Truckload of Cash?*. They'd scooped the jackpot and left Grubtown behind them. 'Have you considered washing the rest of you?' he asked. 'Everything except the cheek? Maybe you could wear a plaster over where you were kissed?'

'Quince hugged me too,' Org reminded them.

I would have told Manual Org to 'Get over it!' but advice like that was probably years – decades – too late ... and Jilly Cheeter was far too well brought up and polite to say such a thing. (Shame on me.)

'Any other reasons why you don't like water?' asked Mango Claptrap.

Manual Org dug a repulsive hand into a repulsive pocket and pulled out a disgusting piece of paper.

'Here,' he said, thrusting it into Mango's hand.

REASONS WHY I HATE WATER
by Manual Org

1. It could wash away Quince's kiss and hug.

2. Mummy flushed Goldie down the loo even though he wasn't dead for sure.

'Goldie was a goldfish?' guessed Mango.

'Precisely.'

'And a loo is a toilet?' asked Jilly.

'Spot on.'

3. Grandpa drowned at sea.

4. Grandma died of thirst in a drought.

5. Fritz was run over by a Water Authority van.

'Fritz was a cat?' asked Mango.

'A housemaid,' said Org. 'One of my favourites.'

'Oh dear,' said Jilly.

Mr Org seemed to have some very good reasons for not liking water.

'I'm sorry,' said Mango.

Just then, a song reached their ears. Five of the seven Grumbly girls were in a rowing boat on the lake. (The lake was used by people who didn't like the idea of rowing in the sea.) The boat would probably have fitted four of them quite comfortably, but five made it a bit of a squeeze. They were singing, **'I Wish I Was a Birdie, Tweeting Up a Tree**'. All the Grumbly girls have very blonde hair which looked almost white in the morning sunlight. With the water such an incredible blue, the scene would have made a great picture.

Manual Org was distracted by the singing. And then by a yelp.

Whether he didn't think twice, didn't stop to think or simply didn't think at all, Mango Org was up off the bench and running to the lake the minute he saw one of the girls fall overboard.

He dived into the water and that was the last anyone ever saw of the repulsive Mr Org.

Chapter Eleven
The end at last

The minute Manual Org's body hit the water, there was a terrible hissing sound and smoke or vapour or some such thing started rising from the surface, followed by terrible bubbles and spurts. What looked like an oil slick spread out across the lake turning the brilliant blue water black and yellow and green. Gas escaped in jets and an awful smell of old egg-and-cress sandwiches filled Brambly Park. Several birds were quite sick and one seagull

even fell out of the sky. I saw it with my own
eyes.

Jilly Cheeter and Mango Claptrap were up
on their feet by now and had already reached
the water's edge. A small crowd gathered to
watch events unfold in horror. They felt so

helpless. Garter, the Grumbly girl who'd fallen out of the rowing boat, had landed on a small mound sticking up out of the water – barely visible – where a duck or moorhen would sometimes snooze on its own. (There wasn't a single bird on the lake that morning,

though.) In the time it had taken the other girls to haul her back in, her pretty white dress (with a pattern of panting puppies on it) was already beginning to dissolve in places, and her red plastic shoes were melting away. The ends of the pink ribbons in her hair were smoking. The girls frantically rowed back to dry land. By the time they'd all five clambered out, the bottom of the rowing boat itself was beginning to disintegrate and the part of the oars that had been in the water had gone altogether.

Jilly Cheeter felt like bursting into tears. What could they do?

At that moment, a totally bald head broke through the surface of the lake and someone – it must have been Manual Org – began swimming ashore. I say 'must have been Manual Org' because who else could it have been? But Jilly and Mango wouldn't have recognised him in a million zillion years. He was no longer repulsive at all.

The man standing in front of us now, wearing nothing more than a picnic rug quickly handed to him, was probably the cleanest person any of us had ever seen. And he was a hero. (Okay, so Garter Grumbly had

managed to get back in the boat without him, but he'd still risked life and limb to save her.) After he'd rinsed himself in the Brambly Park Community Fountain – while everyone politely hummed and turned the other way – the five Grumbly girls threw their arms around him and showered him with kisses. Later, the other two girls who hadn't been there came round to the hospital and kissed him too. And, between them, all seven wrote a song called '**The Man Who Hated Water But Risked Everything To Try To Save A Beautiful Young Girl (Who, It Turned Out, Didn't Actually Need Saving Anyway, But That's Not The Point)**'. It was dreadful. I feel a little bit queasy just thinking about it. I'd rather listen to someone running their fingernails down an old-fashioned blackboard than hear it again. But, as I'm often informed, it's the thought that counts.

The following day, Mayor Flabby Gomez instructed Grabby Hanson to carry out an official investigation into how Ah-Isn't-This-A-Lovely-Spot Lake had become so polluted. In next to no time, he'd uncovered the culprit as being Acrid Scorn. Mr Scorn was instantly awarded a large gold medal and presented with an impressive scroll thanking him for transforming Manual Org from grubby outcast to squeaky-clean shining hero. (Acrid Scorn's brother Lefty was jealous of the scroll because it was even more impressive than the certificate he has in his jeweller's-cum-laundrette.)

The combination of lethal chemicals Acrid Scorn had dumped in the lake had done more than ordinary soap and shampoo could ever have done. In a private conversation in his mayoral office, Flabby Gomez gave Acrid Scorn the secret location of a large hole in the ground which was a much better place to illegally dump hazardous waste, because it would pollute the rivers and soil of *other people's* towns, not ours.

Having given Manual Org a very thorough medical, Dr Fraud pronounced that it was the many years of dirt that had stopped Org from being seriously injured or killed by the cocktail of chemicals in the lake. Instead of losing his skin, he'd simply lost all of his clothes, years of grime and every bump and boil and spot, leaving him a smoothy-skinned lovely (with no hair, not even eyebrows). He then suggested that Mr Org go and see a real doctor for a proper check-up.

Rambo Sanskrit came to Jilly Cheeter's home and informed her that, as official town duck-gatherer, it was in her job description to drain the lake and to fill it with fresh water for the Brambly Park ducks to swim around in. And for no extra pay.

'No it isn't,' she said.

'Yes it is,' he said.

'Then I quit,' she said, which is why Jilly Cheeter is no longer our official duck-gatherer.

'Oh,' said Rambo, and went home.

Mango Claptrap, meanwhile, had gone back to his house to ask his mother about his Great-Aunt Quince and whether she had ever kept a rabbit long before she'd ended up looking like a pickled walnut.

'It's not polite to say that your great-aunt looks like a pickled walnut,' said Mrs Claptrap.

'Why not, if it's true?' asked Mango,

'Because –' said Mrs Claptrap then left it at that because, the truth be told, Great-Aunt Quince did look more like a pickled walnut than anything else she could think of.

The next time Mango's great-aunt came to visit, Mango engineered a meeting between her and Manual Org at Manual

Org's tree, which was now decorated with diamonds, and regularly visited by a whole variety of townsfolk. Mango and Jilly Cheeter went along too.

'Do you think your Great-Aunt Quince really was the same Quince whose rabbit he saved all those years ago?' she asked Mango.

'Probably,' said Mango. 'There can't be that many people called Quince whose parents scooped the jackpot of *Would You Like To Win A Big House, A Big Car and A Truckload of Cash?*.'

'True,' said Jilly.

On meeting, Manual Org and Great-Aunt Quince were both terribly polite to each other, but they didn't have much in common. She talked about rabbits and he showed her the collection of wigs that he'd bought, now that he'd lost all his hair.

'He's a bit too smoothy-skinned for my liking,' she told Mango afterwards.

'She reminded me too much of a pickled walnut,' Manual Org told Jilly afterwards. 'Not that I don't like pickled walnuts.'

And that was that. If this Quince was the same Quince as the Quince he'd loved with all his heart all those years ago — the one who had caused him to vow never to wash again — then all those years apart had changed things. They weren't the same people any more.

Manual Org is now a big part of life in Grubtown. He still calls himself Manual Org, not whatever his name used to be, and he helps out people whenever he can. (He's also improved his diet.) Because all seven of the Grumbly girls kissed and hugged him *before* they knew he was rich, he decided that there was no harm in letting people know that he's a trillionaire (with twelve noughts).

He paid to have The Duck House turned into the fabulous Grubtown Museum, and had a new state-of-the-art custom-built duck house put up nearby. Mrs Awning refuses to set foot in the museum, though, claiming that the building is still haunted by vegetables. Some folk seem to agree with her. Condo Blotch, who became its first cleaner, claims that an enormous beetroot stain appeared overnight on the floor of the 'Interesting Knots' gallery, and even her biggest bottle of Remove-O-Stuff couldn't shift it.

The museum was officially opened at a glittering ceremony, with lots of balloons, by Mayor Flabby Gomez, and Grabby Hanson is in overall charge of security . . . so it's hardly surprising that things go missing once in a while, then turn up again. Only the other week I caught him climbing out of a back window with a display case containing a collection of fairly-rare bottle tops. We nodded to each other in greeting, then went our separate ways.

The star attraction at the museum is in a specially constructed glass case in the entrance foyer. You can't miss it, unless you

This Way Please!

Another word from Beardy Ardagh

When I tell people about events in Grubtown, they usually ask why so many of the townsfolk 'have such silly names'. The obvious answer might be to say, 'Blame their parents,' but I always answer the question with another question: 'What's so silly about them?'

Don't forget that the man who first drew Mickey Mouse in films went by the name of Ub Iwerks — not Walt Disney, by the way — and people didn't laugh and point at *him*. 'Silly' is in the eye — ear, or nose — of the beholder.

If, for some strange reason, you'd like to write to me about **Grubtown TaLes**, please address the envelope:

Beardy Ardagh,
c/o Faber & Faber,
Bloomsbury House
74–77 Great Russell Street,
London,
WC1B 3DA.

and write **Grubtown TaLes** in the bottom left-hand corner. **DON'T FORGET TO INCLUDE A STAMPED SELF-ADDRESSED ENVELOPE** if you're hoping for a reply. Not that I can promise you'll get one. I have a beard to comb, bread to spread, and books to write. I'm a busy man!

(Just some of) the folk who pop up in GRuBtoWN taLes

Jilly Cheeter girl and official duck-gatherer

Mango Claptrap a short boy in short trousers, whatever the weather

Manual Org a repulsive fellow

Flabby Gomez Mayor of Grubtown

Kumquat 'Grabby' Hanson the chief of police

The Grumbly girls the seven Grumbly daughters

Hacking-Cough Gomez the mayor's brother

Big Man Gomez the mayor's dead dad

Pritt Gomez the mayor's wife

Tundra Gomez the mayor's son and heir

Formal Dripping official village idiot for the
nearby village of Werty

**Derek, Bunty, Shaun, Mantle, Fastbuck &
Garrideb Fox** the duck-hating Fox family of
humans (not foxes)

Rambo Sanskrit council job-giver-outer

Sonia Pipkin local builder

The troll inhabitant of Beardy Ardagh's airing
cupboard

Mrs Awning town accident-waiting-to-happen,
first name unknown

Minty Glibb owner of Minty's Cake Shop

Mickey 'Steamroller' Johnson doughnut-
loving steamroller driver

Leggy Prune the future Mrs Johnson

Mrs Johnson the former Leggy Prune

Constable Gelatine a police sergeant

Mustard Tripwire an officer of the law and Gelatine's nephew

Galaxy Tripwire a train driver and former beauty queen

Relish Tripwire a tropical fish salesperson

Informative Boothe a very knowledgeable chap

Hobo Browne a gentleman of the road/smelly tramp

Camshaft Thrift owner of The Rusty Dolphin Cafe

Farflung Heaps self-appointed leader of an angry mob

Garlic Hamper the lighthouse keeper

Shoona Loose the world-famous singer who does a lot for animal charities

Tawdry Hipbone movie star

Snooks Miss Hipbone's pampered pooch

Luminous Shard bald heckler and mechanic

Carlo Monte the riverboat gambler

Lefty Scorn proprietor of Scorn's Laundrette
& Jeweller's

Acrid Scorn an irresponsible dumper of
hazardous waste

Jip the town pelican (official mascot)

Marley Gripe a painter of signs

Dr Fraud a pretend doctor (but he's cheap)

Sloop Cheeter Jilly's dad

Harvey the Cheeter family dog

Furl Claptrap Mango's dad

Carport Claptrap Mango's mum

Vestige Claptrap Mango's brother

Claws their cat

Partial Coggs Grubtown's resident artist

Slackjaw Gumshoe paint & hardware store owner

Purple Outing very rich owner of Purple Outing's Music Shack

Hind-Leg Outing amongst other things, mother of Purple's vast number of children

Wide Brim Petty-Mandrake a regular complainer

Hetty Glue-Pen cinema manager and projectionist

Condo Blotch former cleaner now head of her very own keep-fit and health-food empire

Emily Blotch Condo's daughter

Free-Kick leader of the escaped lab rats

Lulu Free-Kick's mate for life

Hardfast Tendril Grubtown Forest's chief forester

Careworn Wormwood nine-day king of Grubtown

Glowering Silt general manager of Fettle's hotel

Avid Folklore manager of Fettle's hotel

Chevvy Offal owner of Offal's Sunbeds

Premix Stipend victim of one of Offal's sunbeds

Hybrid Byword the (now dead) TV chef

Limbo Goulash an office worker

Clam Wretching founder of Wretching's Dairy

Barton Wretching her son and current owner of the dairy

Beardy Ardagh honoured citizen of Grubtown and the teller of these tales

The delightful Beardy Ardagh tells of other GRuBtoWN taLes

Okay! Okay! If you stop pestering me, I'll tell you about some of the other Grubtown Tales, as long as you tell all your friends about them. (And make sure that they rush out and gather them by the armful.) It goes without saying that they'll all excellent, and that Jilly Cheeter and Mango Claptrap turn up in them somewhere along the way. If you find any beard hairs amongst the pages, don't blame me. You can't prove that they're mine. There are a lot of hairy booksellers and librarians out there.

Now, read on . . .

GRuBtoWN taLes

Book Two

The YeaR That It RaiNed Cows

or

That Well-Known Secret Door

A startled cow falling out of nowhere on to Limbo Goulash while he's riding Marley Gripe's bicycle marks the start of a chain of events strange even by Grubtown's standards. Soon damaged property includes Purple Outing's Music Shack and Minty Glibb's attempt at the world's largest (strawberry) jelly-trifle. With Mayor Flabby Gomez throwing a wobbly, all chief of police, Grabby Hanson, can do is have the cow-fearing townsfolk watch the skies. Underground, meanwhile, there lies another big surprise.

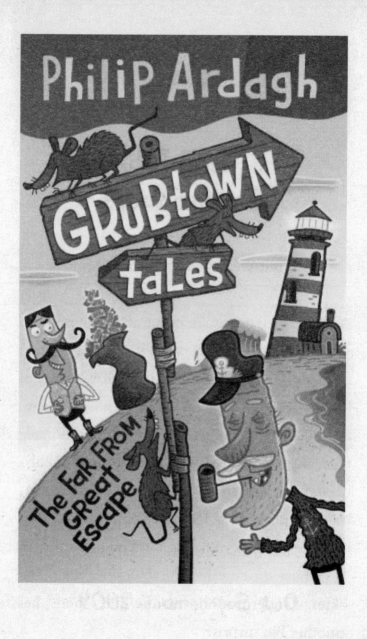

GRuBtoWN taLes

Book Three

The FaR FRoM GReat EscaPe

or

The Light, the Swith and the Wardrobe

When the local lighthouse is plunged into darkness and a ship runs aground – flattening The Rusty Dolphin – it's hard to imagine things can get much worse in Grubtown. But then there's a jailbreak and the Police Department (all three of them) needs all the help it can get from the (often bonkers) townsfolk. No wonder more trouble is waiting just around the corner.

Out September 2009

AT A LOOSE END?

Visit

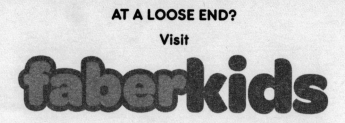

Win stuff – great competitions each month.

Have your say – join the kidszone panel and have your say about your likes, dislikes and what you've been reading.

Play games – visit our microsites and play our addictive games Nut Ding, Manic Mundi and The Parliament of Blood. More coming soon!

More stuff – read extracts from our latest books, listen to audio clips, find out about your favourite authors and much more.

It's all at:
www.faberkids.co.uk

Just read a Faber book? Let us know what you think. Send your review to kidszone@faber.co.uk. Your review might feature on the website and will be entered for our review of the month competition.